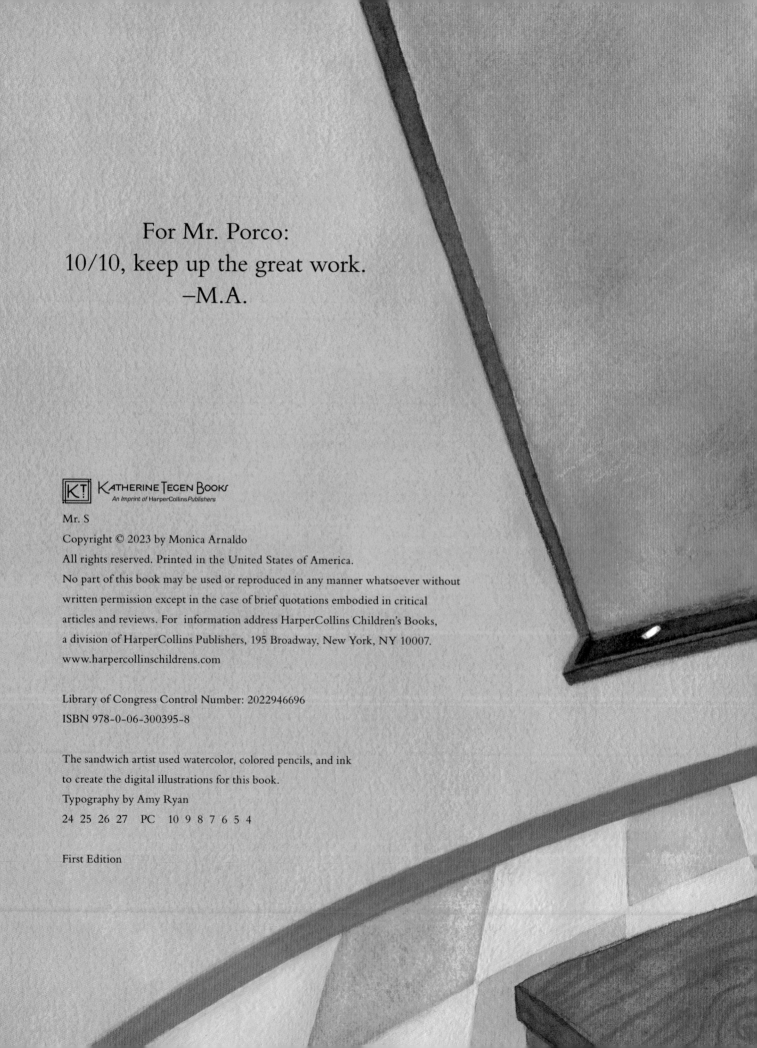

For Mr. Porco:
10/10, keep up the great work.
—M.A.

**KT** KATHERINE TEGEN BOOKS
*An Imprint of HarperCollins Publishers*

Mr. S

Library of Congress Control Number: 2022946696
ISBN 978-0-06-300395-8

The sandwich artist used watercolor, colored pencils, and ink
to create the digital illustrations for this book.
Typography by Amy Ryan
24 25 26 27  PC  10 9 8 7 6 5 4

First Edition

The kids in room 2B could tell something was wrong. Even though it was their very first time at school, they had the sense that something was missing.

"Where's the teacher?" someone whispered.

"Shouldn't they be here by now?" asked someone else.

The children looked at each other and then back
toward the front of the class.

Where there should have been a teacher,
there was only:
    a stack of papers,
        a mug of coffee,
            and an impressive-looking sandwich.

"No teacher means no rules!" cheered half the class.

"Absolutely not!" scolded the other half.

But before they could argue any further, a loud

# THWACK!

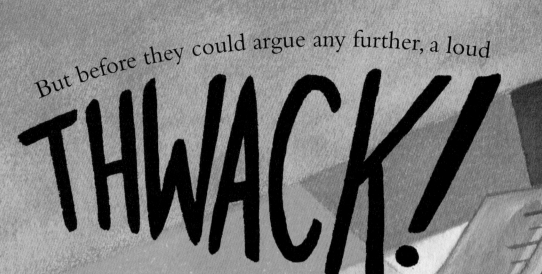

came from the front
of the room, as a ruler
clattered to the ground.

"Who did that?" the kids whispered,
eyeing the teacher's desk nervously.

But there was only
the sandwich.

The clock ticked and the mug steamed,
but the sandwich lay remarkably still.

"You don't think . . ." said one half of the class.

"...Don't be ridiculous," said the other.

"Look!" called a kid from the back of the room, pointing to the chalkboard.

There, written in perfectly neat handwriting, was a name:

As one, the children murmured:

That settled it.

Everyone got straight to work.

They moved swiftly through the day's lessons.

Mr. S was tough but fair.

i WILL NOT

THROW

FOOD

The kids all loved art class.

Next page, please...

Story time ran a bit long.

Music class was especially unconventional.

Mary had a little ham, on some nice rye bread~

As the day went on, some students began to wonder:

Is there something ... unusual about Mr. S?

We've never had a teacher like him.

The children argued quietly, and then not so quietly.

STAFF ROOM
PIANO TEACHERS,
SALSA TEACHERS...
COMPUTER TEACHERS!

SLAM

Suddenly the door burst open.

The children in room 2B were perfectly silent as a very wet man made his way to the front of the class.

"Children," said the man, whose jacket was smoking as though it had recently been on fire, "I'm so sorry I'm late."

The kids blinked at one another.

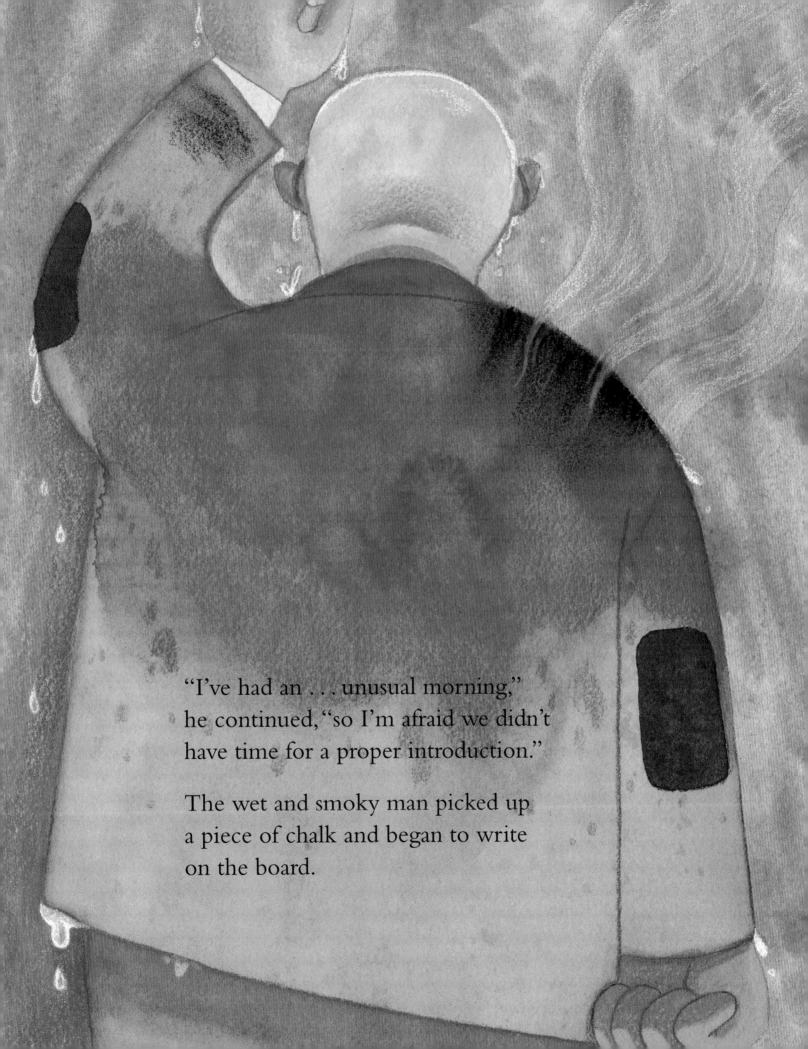

"I've had an . . . unusual morning,"
he continued, "so I'm afraid we didn't
have time for a proper introduction."

The wet and smoky man picked up
a piece of chalk and began to write
on the board.

The children's eyes darted
                    back
                        and
                            forth
between the two figures at the front of the class.

"I'm

Mr. Spencer

Your . . ."

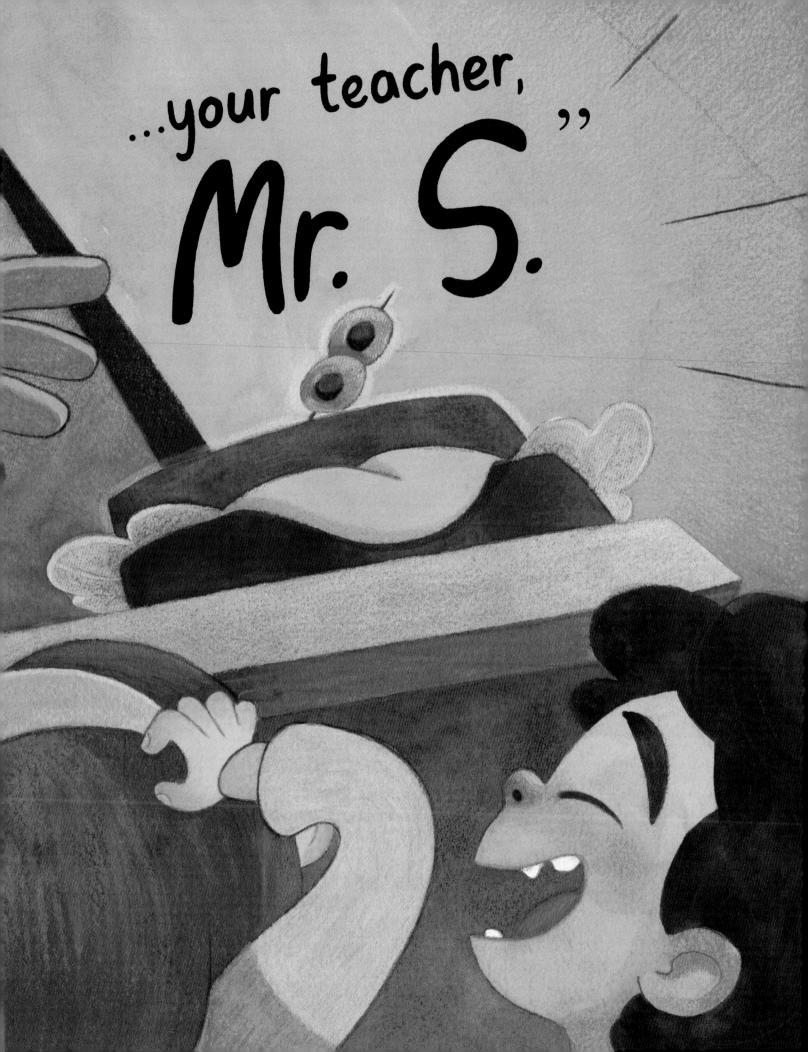

Keep up the great work, everyone. I can tell this is a special group.

Looking around the room, the children had to agree.

We never doubted you, Mr. Sandwich!

said half the class.

Well, maybe just for a minute...

said the other half.

Mr. S was as composed as ever.

"That's quite all right, children. But
actually my name isn't Mr. Sandwich.

"The S stands for—"

avaliere

Ms. Hubbard

Mrs. Levick

ameron

Ms. Cho

Mr. San

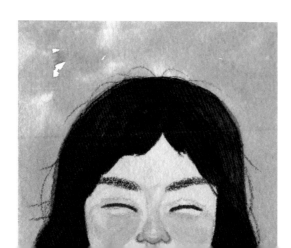